PLAYS FOR PERFORMANCE

A series designed for
contemporary production and study
Edited by
Nicholas Rudall and Bernard Sahlins

The Mysteries: The Passion

A New Adaptation
by Bernard Sahlins
of the Medieval Mystery Play

Ivan R. Dee
CHICAGO

Library of Congress Cataloging-in-Publication Data:
Sahlins, Bernard.
    The mysteries—The Passion / in a new adaptation by Bernard Sahlins.
       p.   cm. — (Plays for performance)
      ISBN 1-56663-023-1. — ISBN 1-56663-024-x (pbk.)
      1. Jesus Christ—Drama. 2. Bible. N.T.—History of Biblical events—Drama. 3. Mysteries and miracle-plays, English—Adaptations. 4. Passion-plays—Adaptations. I. Title. II. Title: Passion. III. Series.
PR6069.A415M93   1993
822'.914—dc20   93-7489

INTRODUCTION

by Bernard Sahlins and Nicholas Rudall

As adapted from the plays found in the entire series of Medieval Mystery Cycles, *The Passion* poses a number of problems of staging. At Court Theatre our earlier production of *Creation* adopted the convention that these biblical stories were being staged by working people. Props and set units were made from found objects; costumes were those of contemporary laborers. (See our introduction to *The Mysteries: Creation* [Ivan R. Dee, 1992]). *The Passion* differs from *Creation* in several important aspects: (1) It plays as a continuous narrative rather than a series of self-contained playlets. (2) It is almost cinematic as it crosscuts from scene to scene and locale to locale. (3) It is urban and public rather than rural and private.

We therefore made the following decisions. The costumes had a fairly sophisticated feel—colors of creams and browns, jackets and slacks and simple shift dresses. We used the entire playing area as a fluid space, defining the locale by lights and physical action. The original music composed for the production reinforced these staging choices.

The attraction of both *Creation* and *The Passion* is that they demand theatrical invention. They can and should be adapted to the strictures of space and the numbers of actors. Our production made

3

specific choices which may serve as an aid to other productions.

The opening scene is a baptism. All members of the cast except Lucifer assembled and formed the banks of the River Jordan. As music played they performed ritual washing, and John the Baptist baptized the foreheads of some of those present. Jesus arrived and walked through the waters. Through a series of gestures with his hands he taught the assembly the meaning of baptism. Then he fell backward into the arms of four participants and was laid in the water as the actors formed the waves of the river. Thereafter a series of individual baptisms occurred throughout the playing area. The whole sequence took about eight minutes. It is not feasible here to describe the details of this very beautiful scenario, but it suggests an approach to the text that is nonliteral.

In fact we determined to depend largely on the actors to create the deserts, streets, and hills of this world. There were only two central props—a table and a white cloth. The table was made with a central removable leaf and a base which, when disassembled, could become the cross. The cloth was used to create the illusion of Christ's transfiguration, the bedsheet of the woman taken in adultery, the tablecloth of the Last Supper, and Christ's shroud.

The table served as the "boardroom" of Lucifer and his devils who were portrayed as businessmen in evening dress. It also served as a mountain during the temptation of Christ in the desert. The white cloth was used in the transfiguration in the following way: it was held taut and high while Christ, back lit, pressed his face and body into it—reminiscent of the shroud of Turin—and then it became his robe.

4

Thereafter the table became the bedroom, and the cloth the sheet of the woman taken in adultery. The central battle between Lucifer and John the Baptist was conceived as a political campaign with attendant secret service agents, front men, and so forth. Pontius Pilate as a foreign occupier was dressed in a uniform suggestive of Desert Storm. The Last Supper was created by elongating the table, covering it with the cloth, and briefly striking the pose of Leonardo's painting. Mary Magdalen was exorcised by being raised into the air by three of the disciples after a balletic leap.

Since in our production Pilate's guards carried batons, Christ was "lashed" in a brief scene that recalled the Rodney King incident.

The table was then disassembled; the support structure became the tomb and the base became the cross. Christ was attached to the cross through preexisting thongs and an attachable base for his feet. The nailing was emotionally reinforced by actors beating in unison on the audience's bleachers. The cross was raised by four supporting ropes.

In the final Hell scene the actors entered as though they were members of a chain gang, holding on to two long ropes. They were forced to sit and haul on these ropes, back and forth, like slaves in the hull of a ship. In the final battle, Lucifer and Christ pulled on either end in a struggle for possession of their souls. When Christ finally released them they each carried a lighted candle and departed.

This brief account is only meant to suggest how the text may be addressed. Clearly it demands the theatrical invention of the designers, actors, and director. But there are two other critical elements: choreography and music. The choreographer must create the baptism, the "streets of Jerusalem," and

5

the scene in Hell. We choreographed the streets of Jerusalem first as a milling crowd that danced a rejection of the woman taken in adultery until she found her young man. And before the "campaign" the streets were filled with jugglers, fire-eaters, stilt walkers, and so on.

The music is even more important. We created our own and infused into a jazz, folk, and country score American spirituals and some deeply moving original songs. The music was composed by Larry Schanker and supplemented by the band led by Willy Schwartz and Miriam Sturm. The score is available on request.

The world premiere of the American adaptation of *The Passion* was first performed at Rockefeller Memorial Chapel at the University of Chicago by Court Theatre on January 17, 1993. The production was directed by Nicholas Rudall and Bernard Sahlins.

CAST

GABRIEL	Dexter Zollicoffer
JOHN THE BAPTIST / NOAH	Rob Riley
JESUS	Philip E. Johnson
LUCIFER	Johnny Lee Davenport
DEVILS	Kymberly Harris, Ric Kraus, Dori Ling, Dan Payne, Horatio Sanz, Jerry Saslow
BEELZEBUB / JUDAS	Kyle Colerider-Krugh
PETER	Gavin Witt
JAMES	Tom Higgins
JOHN THE APOSTLE	John Alcott
PHARISEE	Ric Kraus
PHARISEE / PILATE	Juan Ramirez
ADULTERER / ADVISER / ADAM	John Schroeder
WOMAN TAKEN IN ADULTERY / PROCULA	Kate Buddeke
ANNAS / GOD	Matt DeCaro

CAIPHAS / ABRAHAM	Robert C. Torri
MARY MAGDALEN / EVE	Jennifer Roberts
MARY	Shanesia Davis
ADVISER	Jerry Saslow
SOLDIERS	Tom Higgins, Dan Payne, Rob Riley, Horatio Sanz, Gavin Witt

THE COMPANY

John Alcott, Kate Buddeke, Kyle Colerider-Krugh, Johnny Lee Davenport, Shanesia Davis, Matt De-Caro, Kymberly Harris, Tom Higgins, Philip E. Johnson, Ric Kraus, Dori Ling, Dan Payne, Juan Ramirez, Rob Riley, Jennifer Roberts, Horatio Sanz, Jerry Saslow, John Schroeder, Robert C. Torri, Gavin Witt, Dexter Zollicoffer

THE BAND

Michael Bodeen, Brian Gephart, Willy Schwartz (conductor), Jon Spiegel, Miriam Sturm, Nathan Sturm

Mary Griswold and Fortuna Taxi, Scenic and Costume Designers; Michael Philippi, Lighting Designer; Robert Neuhaus, Sound Designer; Timothy O'Slynne, Choreographer and Movement Director; Larry Schanker, Composer and Musical Director; Lavinia Henley, Stage Manager; Lisa L. Abbott, Assistant Stage Manager

The Mysteries: The Passion

The stage for The Passion *consists of a large central scaffold and a number of smaller scaffolds, preferably curtained. (Heaven is traditionally in the east; hell to the north.) Scenes can occur on the scaffoldings or below. Often two or more actions proceed simultaneously. In contrast to most of the scenes in* Creation, *much of* The Passion *is public, thronging and open, noisy and bustling, with crowds milling about.*

John the Baptist (who traditionally wore a coat of camel skin, often with the head of the animal hanging down) and a group of Christians are assembled at the River Jordan. The lighting also picks out the large scaffold on which Satan, Beelzebub, Belyard, and other Devils are sitting at a boardroom table dressed in formal clothes. This is indeed a board of directors' meeting. During the baptism the Devils are not heard.

GABRIEL: When that serpent Adam's sin did scheme
And Paradise lost for all mankind;
God's son was sent, man to redeem,
And in his dire death forgiveness find.

That Madonna's child shall cause great cure,
Confront the devil in fen and field,
And boldly best that cursed creature,
Mankind to save; Christ's breast, the shield.

For Christ that shall die, all must know
That in him be no iniquity,
That hell may hold him by no intention,
But that he may pass at his liberty,
And his death, for man's death, shall be
    redemption.

11

Thou John, take heed what I shall say:
I tell thee tidings wondrous good:
My Lord Jesus shall come this day
From Galilee to this fair flood
Ye Jordan call,
Baptism to take as is good;
Great day of all.

JOHN: I thank him dear, but I do dread;
I feel most fearful to fulfill
This deed certain.
For we well know, baptism is meant to clear and
cleanse a man of sin;
Certain we see such sin is sent
From him, without him or within.
What needs he then
To be baptized for any sin,
Like sinful men?

(Jesus appears—or has been quietly listening)

GABRIEL: Behold! God's well-beloved child,
O'er whom is his spirit overspread!
Know you well, his own John mild,
That righteousness be more than said
In word alone, but done in deed.

JESUS: The cause why I would baptized be
Is therefore this:
No man now may unbaptized go
To boundless bliss.
And since now I am of mankind,
Men shall of me their mirror make
And mark my doing in their mind.
Thus I blessed baptism take.

JOHN: Now guide me, God, my way to find.

(starts the baptism)

12

Jesus, my Lord of mights the most,
I baptize thee in the name of the Father, and of
the Son, and of the Holy Ghost.

*(John baptizes Jesus. The dove of the Holy Spirit
descends as the Angels sing Veni Creator Spiritus.)*

JESUS: I grant thee John for thy travail
A blessed boon: in bliss to bide,
And to all here who trust my tale
And saw me not yet glorified.

Now to the deep desert I wend my way
For all man's sake, in exile be
Forty nights and days on end.
Nor eat nor drink in no degree.

(all exit but John)

JOHN: *(to audience)* I love this Lord as sovereign
leech
That sucks to salve men of their sore.
As he commandest, I shall preach
Now, teach to every man that lore
Forbid before.
Now may that babe that Mary bore
Bless you e'ermore.

*(Lucifer gavels his group to order. The Devils are
unruly, and he pounds his gavel several times before
bringing them to order.)*

LUCIFER: Now, Belyard and Beelzebub, my well
worthy devils of Hell,
And coolest of council amongst all met here;
Heed now what I tell.

BELYARD: Say on, Satan, sweet sovereign, Sir, with
whom well we dwell,
Obedient at thy bidding; to thee bow we here.

BEELZEBUB: If thou have any wish for our wise
    counsel,
Tell us now thy trouble, say all thou fear.
We stand with thee, here in hell.

LUCIFER: Know, from the first time that I fell,
For my false pride, from heaven to hell,
Ceaselessly I set myself to tell
Among mankind,
How I in dread shall have them dwell,
Their fate, unkind.
So every soul that has since been born
Belongs to me, both night and morn;
From all hope they are forever torn,
And none shall find.

(shouts of approval and "hear hear" from the Devils)

But now some men speak of a swain,
Who preaches peace and suffers pain;
How by his death to bliss again
They will be brought.

BEELZEBUB: Yea. Born in Bethlehem, it is said,
And many say God's son he is;
Born of a woman, a clean maid,
Ever babbling of heaven's bliss.

BELYARD: If indeed he be God's child
And born the son of man,
Then our fate be woe, and wild
And short shall be our span.
He'll cast a curse on what we won.
Our great good days shall soon be gone.

(general expressions of anxiety...Lucifer gavels for order)

BEELZEBUB: But truth, this tale's but a trick, and
    vain.

14

LUCIFER: I trust it nought. I know he is but weak,
This cheap churl whom all should scorn;
Know that him great sorrows do ceaseless seek.
Since he was born,
He suffers many plots and pain.

BEELZEBUB: To tempt him I believe is best;
With subtle snares to sin him bring,
And when he passeth not thy test,
Then is he not of man the king.

LUCIFER: Good. With this advice I am impressed.
I go at once to try this thing.

(The Wilderness. Christ is at the top of the temple—one of the scaffolds.)

BELYARD: All the devils that dwell in hell
Shall pray for thee as I thee tell,
That thou mayst speed thy journey well.
In comfort go, our own king.

(song)

JESUS: Forty days and nights in this sere site
Have I suffered sore for all man's sake;
Great hunger gnaweth me.
Neither bread, nor morsel day or night,
Or no thing to drink then did I take;
Thus pain I, man, for thee.
For thy gluttony and sins so wrong,
I suffer with this hunger strong.
I am afraid it will be long
Ere thou do this for me.

(Lucifer appears, disguised as a friar, and shoulders his way through the audience)

LUCIFER: Make room! Be alive! And move along.
What makes here all this throng?
Hie you hence. High might you hang,

With a rope, right?
We'll stop to joke and sing a song
Some other night.

(sees Christ standing at the topmost tower of the temple)

LUCIFER: Ah, friend,
Thou has fasted long, I know.
I wish I could thee some food show
For old acquaintance us between;
Remember now?
This shall no man know what I mean
But I and thou.
So thou witty man and wise of head,
If you know ought of Godhead
Bid now these stones be made bread.
Betwixt us two,
Then may they stand thee in good stead,
And others too.

JESUS: My father, that all sorrow may slake,
Keep me far from this villainy,
Help me this temptation to take
From mine enemy.

Thou wicked worm, thy wits are gone,
Written is it for all to see:
A man lives not by bread alone.
God's word is food for me.

(Lucifer gives a sign)

LUCIFER: Fie! Such talk I did not think to hear;
He hungers not so much I fear.
I shall test him in this new way
To make him fall,
And if he be God's son, say,
Surely I shall.
Now list to me a little space;
If thou be God's son full of grace,

16

Show us some sign here in this place
To prove thy might.
Let's see... Ah! Jump down from your place
Upon that height.
For it is written; the angels bright
That live in heaven, thy father's hall,
Shall be full ready to break thy fall,
Thus test your might.

JESUS: Away, warlock, thy words all vain;
For written it is full clear and plain,
"Thy God thou shalt not tempt with pain
Nor with discord,
Nor quarrel shalt thou maintain against thy
Lord."

(Jesus comes down)

LUCIFER: What! My words he does not heed.
I will try his greed.

(Lucifer leads Jesus to a mountain)

Friend, I promise thee, even now
And ere I go,
That if thou to me would but bow,
Rich shall ye grow.
For I have all this world to wield,
Tower and town, forest and field;
This as gift I give to thee
For evermore,
If you will kneel and honor me
As I said ere.

JESUS: Cease of thy saws, thou Sathanas.
I grant no thing that you me ask.
To hole of hell hie thee I bid.
There swiftly wend.
And dwell in dread, as thou e'er did,
Without an end.

LUCIFER: Out, out harrow. Alas! Alas!
I wonder what sore soul this is.
I cannot tempt him to trespass,
Nor to no sin to be done amiss.
What that he is I cannot see
Whether God or man, what that he be
I cannot tell, in no degree.

This churl,
He musters all the might he has.
High might he hang!
My way is clear. Now I must pass
To torments strong.

(to audience) To you I leave my testament
To all that in my presence sit
To all those here, by my intent
Do I bequeath the shit. *(exits)*

JESUS: *(praying)* I thank thee, Lord. Through thy
great grace,
This fiend, who would thy word abase,
O'ercame I here.

Now will I wend, man to teach
That word, tell him how all may reach
Thy heaven dear.

(Jesus starts a journey. He is joined by Peter, James, and John.)

JESUS: Peter, disciple and my friend,
And James and John, my cousins fair,
Through God's Grace I did not bend
The devil's wiles full did I bear....

PETER: Then that fiend did thy destruction swear?

JESUS: Yea, but back to hell I did him send.

Now must I well myself prepare
To bring God's word now do I wend.

My father sent me, man to save
All his ransom myself must pay;
Thou way be hard, and goal be grave
Yet to my father I say never nay.

PETER: My Lord come to us what may
We come to go with thee.

(Jesus sets out. The disciples are about to follow when, before them, his robe slips away to reveal shining white garments and, as he turns, a gold mask covers his face.)

PETER: Brethren, what may yon brightness be?
No blaze before so bright has been.
It mars my might; I may not see;
So wondrous thing were never seen.

JOHN: His clothing clean, white as snow,
His face shines as the sun.
To speak with him I have great awe;
Such doing before was never done.

JESUS: My dear disciples, dread thou nought,
I am thy sovereign certainly.
This wondrous work that here is wrought
Is of my father almighty.

Come now, brothers, come thou with me,
God's word to bring, man to fulfill.
To towns and villages now travel we
To teach God's truth, as is his will.

(they move on)

(song)

19

THE WOMAN TAKEN IN ADULTERY

*The woman, a whore, picks up a young man and takes
him into her house.*

*Lucifer, disguised as a scribe, watches this, then ad-
dresses two Pharisees.*

LUCIFER: Fellow pharisees,
  Alas, our sacred laws are lorn.
  A haughty hypocrite, Jesus by name,
  That of a shepherd's daughter was born;
  Lo! our laws he does defame.

PHARISEE 2: Who are you, sir? I know you not,
  Though your words do well persuade.

LUCIFER: I, I am but a simple scribe, here only you
    to aid.

PHARISEE 1: Sir scribe, in faith, that hypocrite
  Corrupts this land with lying lore.

LUCIFER: I counsel, that we him now indict,
  And chastise him right well therefore.

PHARISEE 2: How then catch him in some way
  Before we see another day?

LUCIFER: A false charge must we maintain,
  That hypocrite to bear the blame;
  Then all will his preaching disdain
  And then his worship will turn to shame.
  Hark ye, sirs, now listen well;
  A fair young whore not far doth dwell,
  Both fresh and gay upon to look.